my dad took me to OUTER SPACE

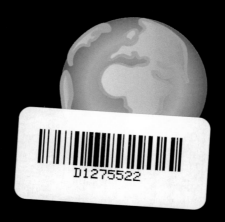

Thanks Mom and Dad for
teaching me to see the world
and navigate through the galaxy.

my dad took me to
OUTER SPACE

Written and Illustrated by Regina Tranfa

We got into a rocket
he had secretly been
building and took
off to Outer Space.

The Space Center was our first stop where we dropped off the rocket and traded it for a space car. Our journey began!

Kids passed us, headed for school,
on space boards that were
fueled by rainbow gas.

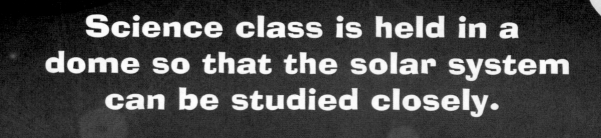

Science class is held in a dome so that the solar system can be studied closely.

Sometimes classwork
requires students to
be sent out in individual
domes to study different
kinds of creatures.

Then all of a sudden we
saw a mysterious site just
floating quietly alone.

...which came from
a lady who stands alone,
playing her violin, to help lost
travelers find their way.

We flew into The Frozen Planet, an ice cream parlor that always has customers!

On the moon we saw green and pink giraffes. There were hippos bathing in moonpools...

...and elephants that put stars into the sky.

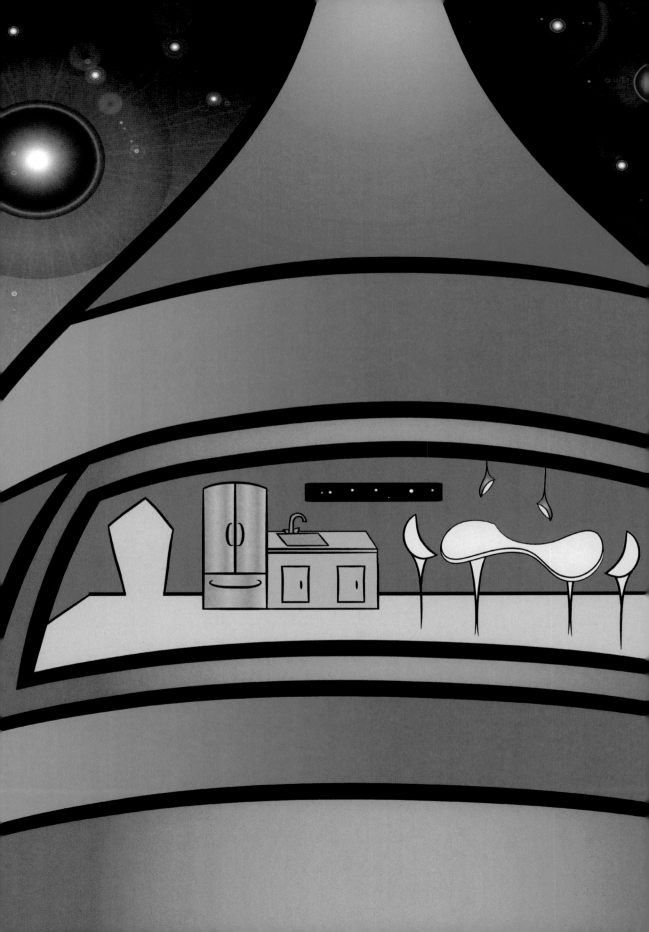

As we flew close to one of
the houses, we were able
to look inside a kitchen.

Too soon it was all over and
we needed to get back
into our rocket!

We headed back
home to Earth.

The next night while looking
through my telescope,
I wondered what else
is out there and what
the future holds.

58636245R00027

Made in the USA
Columbia, SC
22 May 2019